Extinct Monsters

Written by Liz Miles

Collins

Long necks

The biggest extinct monsters
fed on the highest
green treetops.

Some big monsters had green skin.
The green skin kept them hidden.

Wings

This monster went swooping down to scoop up fish.

skin went across the wings

This monster crept along and roosted in trees.

strong wings

sharp feet

Horns and frills

This monster had three horns. It pointed them at hunters.

A frill acted like a screen, stopping attacks. Its throat was hard to stab.

frill

thick skin

Hooks

This little monster ran at high speed.
Hooks jutted from its feet.

pointed hooks
to slash at
throats

It darted at victims and clung on.

Teeth

T-Rex had the speed to swoop and the teeth to kill.

It had strong teeth to rip the throat of its victim.

pointed teeth

Monster shells

This monster stood as big as a car.

Its shell was a shelter.

It swept off attackers by flailing and swinging its sharp tail.

barbs

Monster parts

necks

shells

tails

wings

horns

hooks

teeth

 After reading

Letters and Sounds: Phase 4

Word count: 169

Focus on adjacent consonants with long vowel phonemes, e.g. green

Common exception words: the, some, to, like, was, little, of, by, you, be

Curriculum links: Science: Animals including humans

National Curriculum learning objectives: Reading/word reading: apply phonic knowledge and skills as the route to decode words; read accurately by blending sounds in unfamiliar words containing GPCs that have been taught; Reading/comprehension: understand both the books they can already read accurately and fluently and those they listen to by making inferences on the basis of what is being said and done

Developing fluency

- Read pages 2–3 aloud to your child, demonstrating an enthusiastic tone.
- Take turns to read the rest of the book, and check your child does not miss the labels. Check they pause before starting a new sentence and notice the comma on page 7.

Phonic practice

- Look at pages 6–7 and look for and sound out words that begin with two or three adjacent consonants. (*f/r/i/ll/s, th/r/ee, s/c/r/ee/n, s/t/o/pp/i/ng, th/r/oa/t, s/t/a/b, s/k/i/n*)
- Take turns to look through the book to find and sound out words with adjacent consonants in the middle or at the end of words. (e.g. *r/oo/s/t/e/d, p/oi/n/t/e/d*)

Extending vocabulary

- Challenge your child to suggest two words or phrases with opposite meanings (antonyms) for these:
  - **strong** (e.g. *weak, feeble*)
  - **crept** (e.g. *ran, charged*)
  - **sharp** (e.g. *blunt, flat*)

Comprehension

- Turn to pages 14–15 and ask your child to take the role of an expert on extinct monsters and describe the features in each picture, and why they were useful.